Hunter's Moon

Before Jeff could finish, a brick smashed through the window. Glass fell like rain around them. The fire roared as an icy blast ripped at the curtains.

Neil rushed to pick up the brick. It was wrapped in paper with three words on it in large letters.

There were more letters on the back. And they were scrawled in what looked like blood.

Look out for other exciting
stories in the *Shades* series:

Hunter's Moon

John Townsend

Published by Evans Brothers Limited
2A Portman Mansions
Chiltern St
London W1U 6NR

Reprinted 2007

British Library Cataloguing in Publication Data
Townsend, John
Hunter's moon. - (Shades)
1. Young adult fiction
I. Title
823. 9'14 [J]

ISBN 978 0 237 52647 4

Series Editor: David Orme
Editor: Julia Moffatt
Designer: Rob Walster

Chapter One

Neil was scared – but he didn't know why. Not at first. The dark had never bothered him … until now.

As the trees reached up around him and the wind stirred the bare twigs, he sensed something was there. Something alive. It wasn't far away and it was watching him.

The beam from his torch swept across

the darkness and seeped into the woods.
The deep blackness inside soaked up the
light. He could see nothing, but he knew
something was moving. Dead leaves
crunched. Something was there. An icy
shiver ran down the back of Neil's neck.

He went back to the pile of timber and
took a box of matches from his pocket.
He would feel safer once the bonfire was
burning. A warm glow of orange light
might melt the fear. The matchbox
shook in his clumsy fingers.

As he bent down to strike a match, he
heard scraping behind him. The match
snapped and the spark died. His heart
pounded and his dry throat tightened.
His fingers fumbled for another match –
anything to kill the choking darkness.

Neil felt so stupid. He knew every
inch of those woods. He'd lit bonfires after

dark many times. It was his job to burn the dead wood when all was quiet. He was used to being alone. That's what he liked about being a gamekeeper. He loved the woods and being out in all weathers. He loved the quiet when no one was about. But now he knew he wasn't alone.

The eyes blinked. They flashed tiny sparks of light as flames licked the paper and curled round the dry twigs. The pile of branches was soon alight; hissing, crackling and sparking in the darkness. As the breeze fanned the flames, the whole pile was a blaze of dancing light. Smoke rolled upwards into orange branches and roosting pheasants.

Neil hurled dead leaves into the flames and watched them flare. He turned to peer into the wood – just as the eyes hid behind a tree. Thick smoke swirled into the night and drifted across the moon.

An owl screeched above him and flapped away into the blackness. He turned suddenly – sure the eyes were following his every move. Sure the deep growl was just a few steps away. He spun round in the mud, stumbled and ran in a spray of matches.

The fire fizzed and spat in a final flurry. It soon shrank to a small red puddle of light before dying once and for all, when feet kicked smoking embers into the damp grass. The same feet that prowled each night through silent woods – eyes watching, staring upwards – always upwards – to greet the Hunter's Moon.

Chapter Two

Neil had always wanted to work in the
countryside. He'd helped his uncle most
weekends at one of the shoots nearby.
They paid him to be a beater but he had
soon showed real skills for looking after the
young birds. He had a sharp eye for any
danger to the chicks. If buzzards were nearby
or if a fox was in the woods, he knew

straight away. If a stoat or mink got through the fence, Neil was there like a shot. Nothing escaped his eyes and ears.

Jeff Barnard, the head gamekeeper, was keen to give Neil a job. Jeff was one of those wise old country men who'd worked on the land all his life. He, too, used his eyes and never missed a trick as to what was going on. He was full of old sayings that made Neil laugh.

'You mark my words, lad,' Jeff would say, 'I can tell just what the weather's up to. They always get it wrong on TV. Not me. I use these.' He'd tap his ears and eyes. He was always right, too.

'See the water on the tip of that elder leaf? Tomorrow will be a fine day.'

"Dew in the night, next day will be bright.Grey mist at dawn, the day will be warm."

It was a fine summer day when Jeff said, 'No sunbathing this afternoon if I were you, Neil my lad.'

Neil laughed.

'Fat chance – with all those fence posts to put in. Look at that bright blue sky. This hot weather's set to last, Jeff!'

Jeff shook his head and brushed the wasps from his can of beer.

'Robin knows best. Look at him chirping down on that log. He sang a different tune in that tree last week. When he comes down here, that's a sure sign of rain.'

By two o'clock the storm had already begun. Neil was amazed. Even though he knew a lot about nature, he still had plenty to learn from Jeff.

Neil was upset when Jeff had to stay off work with a bad back after a fall. Jeff had been making a footbridge over the stream when one of the supports had given way. He'd crawled in the wet and dark for hours before he got help.

While Jeff was away, Neil took on all the jobs. He worked all hours, often after dark. That's when he first felt uneasy. Autumn was always a busy time, with plenty of cutting back to do.

'Clearing and burning, my lad. Just keep clearing and burning,' were Jeff's orders. But Neil could do with Jeff being there. Not just to work on a new pheasant pen. For the first time in his life, Neil felt scared in the woods.

What were those weird scratch marks at the base of an oak tree? Deep grooves, like claw marks. And why were there splashes of blood in one of the bird feeders? But there was something else – like a presence.

Something in the trees. Then there was a smell. It was near the broken footbridge. The bridge where Jeff had fallen. Neil sensed fear here. Fear of eyes somewhere in the shadows.

Chapter Three

The girl came like a ghost through the
morning mist. She drifted along the
footpath at the edge of the wood. The
watery sunlight trickled through the trees
and splashed her face. Neil looked up from
raking leaves and was startled by her.
She looked stunning in a swirl of dappled
light and October mist.

'Hi!' she called. For a moment he was speechless.

'Lost your tongue?' She smiled. Her dark eyes sparkled under a sweep of shining black hair. Neil stared for some seconds, first at her face, then slowly down to her muddy jeans and trainers. She read his mind.

'I slipped. It's very wet.'

'Are you lost?' he asked. It seemed a daft thing to say. He wished he hadn't. She certainly didn't seem lost.

'No. Not at all. I remember you.' She smiled again. What a lovely smile, he thought. But who was she? He'd never have forgotten a face like hers. Nor a figure like hers.

'Really?' he said, resting his elbow on the handle of the rake.

'Yeah. You were in the year below me at

school. My friend fancied you.' Neil felt himself blush. He still had no idea who she was.

'Tanya,' she smiled, reading his mind. 'Are there badgers round here?'

'Why do you ask?' He didn't mean to snap at her but he was on his guard now. People who asked about badgers were not to be trusted. Not since a few setts were dug up last month, with all the animals taken off for brutal sport.

'My project.' She waved a pencil. It was only then he saw the sketch-pad under her arm. 'I'm an art student. Wildlife is my thing at the moment. I'd love to see a baby badger.'

'It's not all you might see.' Neil spoke without thinking. The fears of the last few nights were getting to him. But her mind had gone elsewhere.

'And what did you have in mind?' She beamed a cheeky grin as she winked and wagged the pencil at him.

'Oh, nothing,' he said, trying to laugh it off. He felt himself blush again.

She had moved closer and her dark eyes stared into his.

'Do you mean the beast? They're all talking about it at college. They say there's a panther on the loose somewhere round here. Dark and deadly – like me!' She gave a playful snarl and clawed the air.

Neil had heard the rumours. They'd been going round for years. But for the first time he felt something was prowling these woods. He was sure that strong smell by the bridge was from a big cat, marking out its hunting ground. It was like the strong ammonia he'd smelt at the zoo. He was sure the noises in the wood the other night were from a large animal. Then there were the claw marks… He knew a big cat on the prowl could kill someone.

'You look dead serious all of a sudden,' she said. 'You look far better when you smile. Cute, even. I see what my friend meant now. I could fancy you myself. I'm always on the lookout for a sexy guy in wellies!'

She gave a squeal of laughter and threw her head back. Neil laughed too, as she snorted with one hand hiding her mouth and the other brushing hair from her eyes.

Their giggles died and an awkward silence fell, as a sudden gunshot ripped right past them with a terrifying crack, and she screamed.

Chapter Four

The echo rolled out over the hills and hung in the air. Crows sprang from the trees and the sky filled with their startled cries. A figure stood on the bank, his breath steaming as he laughed.

'I bet that woke you both up, eh?'

'You fool!' Tanya shouted back, her face screwed-up with rage.

'My little joke to keep you on your toes.'

The grinning figure walked towards them.

Neil shouted at him, too.

'What do you think you're doing? You could have hit someone firing like that.'

'Cool it, mate. I know what I'm doing. I was aiming for that tree, and that's just what I hit. Bullseye.'

Tanya turned on him, still angry.

'How did you know I was here? Did you follow me?'

'Just keeping my eye on you, Tanya,' he said. 'After all, the beast could be after you.'

It was Joe Linsey from the kennels.

'I see you're having a little chat with my woman. Keep your hands off. We wouldn't like to fall out, would we? Remember me from school?'

Neil couldn't forget. People used to leave

Joe alone. He would stand in the
corner of the yard and preach, often with a
crowd round him. He used to say he was
some sort of prophet. Most people just said
he was mad.

'How could I forget you?' Neil said. 'Still
crazy, I see.'

Tanya smiled again.

'You're dead right. I can't think what I
see in him. I must have a weakness for sexy
wellies!' She roared laughing again.

Joe looked Neil in the eye.

'Have you seen this big cat thing? The
panther on the loose. The sign of the beast
is always with us.'

Tanya rolled her eyes.

'Oh, here he goes. Preaching again. I tell
you, he's a nutter. He'll start quoting the
Bible now.'

Joe ignored her. 'Joel chapter one, verse

six. "It has the teeth of a lion and the fangs of a lioness." '

Tanya reached for his hand.

'He's mad but he's good with the hounds, aren't you, love?'

'They know I'm boss.' He stroked the barrel of his gun. Neil couldn't understand what Tanya saw in Joe.

'He lets me sketch the hounds. I'm going to the hunt on Saturday. I want to paint a fox.' Tanya said, as if she'd read his mind.

Joe snorted.

'You'll need to use a lot of red when they rip it apart.'

Tanya could see Neil had taken a dislike to Joe.

'You could come and join us, Neil,' she said. 'We meet at The Nelson Inn at 11 o'clock. It's the first hunt of the season.'

Joe sneered.

'He'll be working. He's got to keep these woods safe, from them that trespass. It must be tricky on his own, without his boss. And a tad lonely. When do you get time off?'

Neil didn't like his questions. Why did he want to know?

High above the tree-tops across the river, the crows swarmed like angry flies. Joe's eyes scanned the sky.

'Ah, there it is. Our friend. On wings like eagles.'

A large bird rose above the hills, soaring on the air currents. It circled with outstretched wings as the crows scattered.

'You could sketch that buzzard. That's if Neil lets you get close.'

Neil said nothing. He knew Joe was testing him. It was no buzzard. This bird was bigger, with a forked tail. Neil loved to watch it wheel above the woods, calling to its mate. But it was a rare sight. And Neil alone knew the exact tree where they nested.

The local pair of red kites brought bird watchers from far and wide. But that wasn't all. They brought others, looking for ways to make easy money. Some would pay thousands for eggs, chicks or even a dead adult to stuff in a glass case. Neil knew some hunters were ruthless. He watched Joe's gaze follow the now tiny dot far above them. He knew it was time to be on his guard, particularly against anyone with a gun.

Later that evening Neil saw how right he'd been. Earth and bracken littered the track. Another badger sett had been dug up. It was ripped apart and all the young badgers had gone. Not far away, one of the pheasant pens was damaged. Feathers

lay scattered in the mud, blowing in
flurries in the evening breeze, across the
blood-stained grass.

Chapter Five

Neil had a lot on his mind. He was worried about the strange noises and smells in the woods at night. He was worried about what was killing badgers and pheasants. He was worried about poachers and those who might be after the red kites. He was uneasy about Joe Linsey and his gun. If only Jeff was back at work. He'd know what to do.

But Neil needed some advice now. He
decided to go round to see Jeff.

A cold wind swept across the fields.
It was already dark when Neil left work,
with a pale moon peeping above the trees.
He knew Jeff would say rain was coming.
It was another of his sayings:

"Pale moon does rain, red moon does blow,
White moon does neither rain nor snow."

Sure enough, it was the moon that Jeff first
spoke about.

'On Friday you'll be able to work all
night, my lad. It's Hunter's Moon. The
brightest moon of the year. She'll be
a beauty, too. We're in for a frosty spell
after a drop of rain, and a nasty old
wind tonight.'

Jeff was pale and still in pain. Even so,
he wanted to know all about the jobs Neil
had been doing.

'I hope you're ready for the big shoot at the weekend. We've got to give them good sport this season. This is our last chance.'

Jeff had a lot of money worries lately. He'd had to sell a lot of his sheep. His face showed the strain as he spoke softly, with a slight tremble in his voice.

'You'll take care, won't you Neil?

"Beware the nights of Hunter's Moon,

When all beasts dance to another tune."

'It's an old saying round here. But this year it's Hallowe'en. Take care.'

Neil had never heard Jeff speak like this before. There was a different look in his eyes. Neil felt sorry for him as he lay there looking weak and in pain. Maybe he shouldn't worry Jeff about anything else. He clearly had enough on his plate. But it was Jeff who first spoke about the panther.

'Have you seen any sign of this big cat

on the loose? It's all the gossip again. I wish
I was back on my feet to sort things out.
But I tell you; you need to be on the alert,
Neil. My bit of wood has rich pickings.
Kites, badgers, our pheasants. A good
poacher could strip the lot and be a few
grand the richer. But that's not all…'

Before Jeff could finish, a brick smashed
through the window. Glass fell like rain
around them. The fire roared as an icy blast
ripped at the curtains.

Neil rushed to pick up the brick. It was
wrapped in paper with three words on it in
large letters.

BEWARE HUNTER'S MOON.

There were more letters on the back.

IOE L231

And they were scrawled in what looked like blood.

Chapter Six

A storm later on that night snapped thick
branches like sticks. As soon as it was
light, Neil was in the woods to look for
damage. There was no wind now. All
was deathly still.

Neil's heart sank. A fence was down.
A fallen tree had smashed one of the tool
sheds. Wires were down and power was off

in the village. At least the pheasant pens were still in one piece. Just.

The walnut trees at the edge of the wood were still standing. Neil always kept an eye on those. The timber could sell for thousands of pounds. That was another reason why they had to guard the woods from strangers. Rural crime was now major business for miles around.

Somewhere behind him a twig snapped. Neil looked round. Nothing stirred. His heart raced. Was the creature behind him? He reached down to pick up a stick. Just as he moved he saw a shape on the track. His heart missed a beat. The stick rose in his hand.

A black animal ran towards him in a spray of leaves. For a split second Neil felt a scream rise in his throat. A voice rang out through the trees.

'Here boy!'

The labrador wagged its tail and barked playfully. Neil sighed with relief.

'Here, boy. Don't worry, Neil. He's harmless.' It was Mr Fenby from The Old Manor House. He bent down to pat the dog and clipped a lead on its collar. 'He's a bit excited. He saw something back there. Something big. I'm pretty sure it was the big cat. It made me panic, I can tell you. We'll soon flush it out. The hounds will sort it out.'

Mr Fenby was Master of the Hunt. He was a good horseman. He and his wife kept racehorses, although village gossip said she'd just left him.

'You can't this week, Mr Fenby. Don't forget it's the big shoot.'

Mr Fenby didn't seem to like being told what he couldn't do.

'Shame. I see there are a few trees down, Neil. A nasty storm, eh?'

Neil looked curiously at the bag in Mr Fenby's hand.

'Oh, I hope you don't mind. I'm just getting some breakfast. Don't worry. I've kept to the public path. I haven't gone into Jeff's private wood. There are lots of chestnuts and mushrooms this year. Just the job. By the way, how is Jeff these days?'

'Not too good, I'm afraid. He had a nasty shock last night. Someone hurled a brick through his window. There was a note with some sort of code. Jeff said it might be a car registration number. "JOE L231". Odd.'

'There are some strange people about, Neil. But if it said JOE, I bet he knows something about it. He's got an odd streak, that one. In fact they don't come much odder than him!'

Neil was sure Joe was behind all of
this; the vandalism in the wood and the
brick through Jeff's window. He felt the
anger rising. It was time Joe met his match,
and Neil would be the one to sort him out.
That stick might come in very handy.

Chapter Seven

There was a lot to be done for the shoot
at the weekend. Neil had to phone the
beaters, peg out the drives and work on the
tractor. The shoot had to be a success. If
they had one more bad season, they would
have to close. Others were already trying to
buy the land.

The sun spilled into the wood and

sparkled in the stream. The bridge lay
sprawled on the bank just as it fell
when Jeff had his accident. Neil stood
by the broken timber. He felt uneasy.
He looked over his shoulder. There was
a strange feeling around here. He shivered.

Smashed wood lay on both sides of the
stream. But the posts were still firm. Two
weren't splintered like the others. They had
clean cuts. Someone had sawn through the
supports deliberately. Someone who wanted
to hurt Jeff. Neil was furious.

But worse was to come. Just ahead of
him on the path, Neil glimpsed a sickening
sight. The bright body of a bird lay limply
in a pile of leaves. The red kite was
dead. It had been shot. Neil stroked its
head and swore. His anger exploded. There
was no doubt in his mind: this was Joe's
work. It was time to hit back. Now.

Neil stormed into the kennel yard. Dogs yelped and barked. Joe was cleaning out one of the dog pens.

'I want a word with you, Linsey.' Neil waved the stick above his head. Joe looked up sharply.

'Keep your hair on, mate. And watch who you're shouting at or I'll jump this wall and show you who's boss round here.'

Neil brought the stick down on the wall with a crack. Blood rose in his cheeks and his eyes flashed with fury.

'First you smash stuff in our wood. Then you saw through the bridge. You've torn up badger setts. Now you've shot the kite. You just want to scare us out, don't you? You want to get rid of us so you can get your hands on our woods.'

Neil was seething with anger. He spat his rage into the wind.

Joe jumped the wall.

'Prove it.'

Neil jabbed the stick at his chest.

'And you think you can scare Jeff with a brick and a stupid note about Hunter's Moon. You can't deny it. Your name was on it.'

Joe grabbed Neil's collar.

'Listen, mate. I don't know what you're going on about but I'll give you ten seconds to get off this land.'

Neil carried on.

'Did you write it in the blood of some animal you killed? And what was it meant to mean, JOE L231? Load of tripe.'

Joe paused. He let go of Neil's shirt.

'Interesting,' he said. 'Very interesting.'

A Land Rover pulled up at the furthest end of the drive.

'Sorry, Neil. I can't give you the smack

in the mouth you deserve. You'll have to
wait. That's Mr Fenby come to pick me up.
Some of us have to plan for the hunt. It's a
late breakfast up at The Manor House.
Let's face it, mate, I only deal with class.
Not scum like you and your cheap pheasant
shoot.' He walked off down the drive. After
a few strides he stopped and looked back at
Neil.

'Try a Bible. It's not JOE, you fool. It's
JOEL. Chapter 2, verse 31. That should
make you think!'

He reached the Land Rover, jumped
inside and it roared off in a cloud of blue
smoke. Neil stood and stared till long after
the smoke cleared.

The church door was unlocked. It was dark
inside but Neil found a large Bible near the
door. It took him a long time to find the

book of Joel. He slowly read chapter 2, verse 31.

> *"The sun will be turned to darkness and the moon to blood."*

For a second time that morning a shiver ran down his spine. Tonight was Hunter's Moon. Beware Hunter's Moon. What did it all mean? The church clock clunked. Twelve hollow clangs. Midday. Just twelve hours to go till the Hunter's Moon would turn to blood. The night of Hallowe'en.

Chapter Eight

The air was crisp and clear. All afternoon
Neil had been cutting up fallen branches
with a chainsaw. Now he was ready to light
a bonfire. Taking a box of matches from his
pocket, he bent to light the paper. He
paused as he remembered the other night
when he dropped the whole box. He looked
over his shoulder. He was sure he heard a

sound behind him. He got to his feet and grabbed the chainsaw. He listened, waiting, as the moon climbed into the sky and the first stars glinted above him.

Something was moving through the woods, coming nearer. Neil could only see the grey shapes of tree trunks and feeding pheasants. Suddenly he saw a shadow moving towards him through the stillness. A person. A girl with long dark hair. She was running straight towards him. It was Tanya and she was gasping for breath.

'I knew you'd be here somewhere,' she panted. 'I'm so glad I found you. I need to see you. I've got to tell you something. You can put that chainsaw down now. I'm not the panther!'

Neil smiled.

'Come over here while I light the fire.'

The flames soon flared as the bonfire

crackled to life. Neil poked the branches as sparks showered into the night.

'Go on, then. What is it you need to tell me?'

'It's Joe,' she said. 'He's really ill. I found him this afternoon. He couldn't stand up. I called the ambulance. He told me to come and tell you. Something about Hunter's Moon and walnut trees. It didn't make sense but he said you'd know. He said you must be warned. He said you need to keep watch tonight.'

Neil looked into Tanya's eyes. She wasn't acting. This was real. She clung on to his arm.

'I don't know what's going on but it's something scary. Joe said he was planning to come up here at midnight to get proof. What did he mean?'

Neil said nothing. He didn't want to tell Tanya how he hated Joe. But what Tanya said next took his breath away.

'You're probably wondering why I didn't go with him to hospital.' She paused. 'The thing is … I can't stand him. It's all an act. You could even call me a spy. I'm doing it for the sabs at college.'

Neil frowned. What was she saying?

'You know,' she went on. 'The hunt saboteurs. We're planning a big thing to disrupt the hunt on Saturday. I agreed to get a bit of inside information by chatting up the kennel boy. He fell for my charms a real treat. I came today to get a few names and addresses of Hunt members. It was horrible to find him lying on the floor, but I still hate all he stands for.'

Neil stared into the flames.

'Then you must hate me too. I rear birds for people to kill. I bet you sabs don't like that, do you?'

Tanya touched his knee.

'That's very different from ripping a fox apart. And besides, you're really nice.'

Neil watched the firelight dance in her deep brown eyes. He smiled.

'I'm lost for words. So how about joining me here tonight to see what Joe was so worried about?'

'Is that your normal chatup line? I bet the girls always fall for that one!'

Neil blushed.

'Sorry. It's just that…'

'I'm only teasing,' Tanya pushed him playfully. 'I think you're right. I think we should hide in this wood tonight and see just what this is all about. To find the truth once and for all.'

Chapter Nine

Neil and Tanya sat in the bar next to a
roaring log fire.

'Make the most of this heat,' Neil said.
'It'll be freezing out there tonight.'

'I've got extra layers,' Tanya smiled, 'as
well as a flask of coffee.' She looked over
her shoulder and whispered, 'don't you
think we should tell the police?'

Neil sighed.

'I reported the dead kite today but they can't seem to do much. And what do we tell them? "*We're camping out in the wood tonight because we think something odd is going on. We're after a big cat on the prowl.*" They'll lock us up!'

Tanya sipped her drink.

'Joe's mum phoned. He's still very ill. They pumped out his stomach and he's on a drip. They wouldn't say any more. They do that to people who take an overdose. I'm sure Joe hasn't taken drugs. I know he can be stupid but...'

Neil didn't say anything. He had other ideas. He pointed at her bag.

'What's that poking out with a dirty great bin liner over it?'

Tanya touched her nose.

'That's a secret. I know it's against my

48

beliefs, but I'm not going into those woods without it. I took it from Joe's kitchen. Just in case.'

Neil didn't have to ask. He knew it was a shotgun. He felt relieved they had it. If the big cat really was out there, they might need it.

When they left the pub, the moon was already high in a silver sky. The whole village was bathed in its wash of liquid light. A sharp frost already crept over the trees. A thin crust of ice crawled across the puddles on the track. Neil's boots crunched on them as they entered the woods. Even inside where the trees were thick and tall, the silver light splashed into shimmering pools of moonlight. But the shadows grew deeper, darker, denser… The cloak of night pulling tighter around them. Tanya's hand slipped into Neil's.

'Over there!' Neil pointed with his torch beam, into a thick mass of bushes. 'We can hide in there. We'll be able to see the walnut trees.'

Tanya squeezed his hand.

'I'm really scared. I've got my mobile at the ready. Just in case.'

'Who will you call – Panthers-R-Us?'

Neil looked down at the snaking roots of beech trees. His torch beam danced over the peaty moss.

'What are you looking for? Tracks?' Tanya asked. Neil didn't reply. Something had gone. A part of the jigsaw fell into place in his mind.

Soon they were lying on a plastic sheet, huddled under a sleeping bag. The gun pointed out through the twigs as their eyes scanned the ghostly woods. Their torches were off now. It was almost midnight and an icy silence hung in the smoky greyness.

Enough moonlight seeped across the ground for them to see smudgy shapes. But they heard it first. Long before the dark figure moved through the trees. A scraping noise. The rustle of leaves and the cracking of twigs. Panting. Something being dragged. Grunting.

Neil gripped Tanya's arm as the figure came closer. Or were there two shapes? It was hard to see. There was a thud. The shape moved away again. Silence. Tanya squeezed Neil's hand. They waited. A shrill sound startled them. It was Tanya's watch bleeping midnight. She smothered her wrist and the noise died.

The moon was high overhead now. Its milky light soaked into the earth around them. It seeped through the walnut trees, and on to the advancing figure. The figure of a man, carrying something.

Neil's eyes were fixed on the figure scraping a tool on tree trunks. Tanya could wait no longer. She had to ask Neil what was going on.

'What—?' It wasn't just Neil's grip on her arm that stopped her. It was the footsteps, coming nearer. Very close. Liquid splashed around them. The smell made their eyes water. Strong ammonia. But that wasn't all. Neil felt drips fall on his hand. He looked down. It shone in the moonlight. He felt sick. His hand was covered in blood. He thought of the words he'd read earlier. The words from Joel. Had they come true?

The sun had turned to darkness, and the moon to blood.

Chapter Ten

The figure began to dig. The moon shone more brightly than ever. His spade glinted silver. The frozen earth crunched with each blow of the spade.

'Can you see who he is?' Neil said, but he had a good idea already. It was all starting to make sense. He'd have to find out if he was right. He stood up.

'I'm going down there,' he said. 'Keep watch – but keep out of sight.' He slowly crept from tree to tree.

The man stopped digging every so often to look around. Neil kept to the shadows just a few metres away. The hole in the ground was the size of a grave. Neil stepped forward. His heart thumped like never before. He was about to speak when the man turned and lunged at Neil with the spade.

Neil fell with a blinding crack as the spade sliced into his shoulder. The man lifted the spade like an axe above his head. He was about to bring it down to finish Neil off for good. But then the shot hit him as a loud crack ripped through the night. He staggered and fell, sinking into the soft pile of earth. He slumped, with a throaty growl. Tanya's finger squeezed the trigger again. As he lay panting among the twisted roots he howled. Like a beast. Like a hunted tiger bathed by the light of Hunter's Moon.

Chapter Eleven

The morning mist drifted across the valley.
Jeff looked from his window and gave a
sigh. A dead sheep lay in his field. Its
throat was torn and there were deep claw
marks across its back. He turned towards
the sofa.

'It happened last night. No panther –
just your friend with his iron claw. At least

you stopped him in his tracks.'

He rubbed his back. It was already much better. 'I'll put the kettle on.'

'I'll do it,' Tanya jumped to her feet. 'What about you, Neil?'

'Yeah, fine.' He was still dazed from lack of sleep and the blow to his shoulder. He'd had stitches and now wore a sling for a smashed collar bone. Then there had been all the police questions. He'd only slept for an hour or so.

Today was the day of the shoot. Jeff had told him to forget work. Neil needed rest and besides, the police would be searching the woods. Jeff sighed again.

'Shame Tanya won't come shooting, seeing as she's such a good shot. A pity you didn't finish him off. I would have done. You only gave him a couple of flesh wounds. Not enough to stop him running off. Let's hope the police have picked him up by now.'

'Yeah. But she saved me. Too bad we were too late to save his wife.'

Neil began the full story. The story of Mr Fenby from The Old Manor House. The Master of the Hunt. The man with the dark secret. The one who threw the brick to scare them off. Who'd tried to stop them finding out the grisly truth.

'Fenby killed his wife. He couldn't bury her on his own land in case the police came looking. So where's the next best place? The woods. How did he make sure people didn't go snooping about and find out what he was up to? He made up the panther story. He used an iron claw to scratch the trees. He splashed blood about. He killed the odd pheasant or sheep. He wrecked the bridge to get Jeff out the way.

He threw ammonia about to smell like panther pee. Strong enough to keep dogs from digging her up.'

'And do you know why he waited till Hunter's Moon to bury his wife?' Jeff asked. 'It's the only night of the year when it's light enough to see in those woods without a torch. A torch can be seen from the track. He couldn't take the risk of being caught red-handed.'

'It was Joe who got wind of what was going on,' Tanya said. 'That's why Fenby got him round for a meal. To poison him.'

Neil lay back on the sofa.

'Poison from under our beech trees. They may look like harmless mushrooms. But popped on a plate with a bit of bacon… It could have killed Joe. Death cap woodland fungus can be just a tad fatal. His mum said they're letting him home today.'

The phone rang and Jeff went into the hall. Neil held Tanya's hand.

'Thanks for everything,' he said. 'You not only saved my life last night, you saved our woods. Fenby wanted that land. He was waiting for us to fail this season. But we're not going to. I'll see to that. And all this big cat nonsense will stop now.'

Tanya smiled and kissed Neil's cheek.

'I'm going to cook a feast for us tonight. For you, Jeff and me.'

Neil laughed.

'No mushrooms, I hope!' He turned to kiss her as Jeff came back in the room. He looked pale.

'That was my son,' he said. 'He comes every night to feed my sheep and check them out. He was held up last night. He didn't get here till gone midnight. All the sheep were fine. Nothing wrong. That can only mean one thing. It wasn't Fenby who killed that sheep. There's something else out there.'

Tanya looked at Neil. He said nothing. The room fell very quiet.

'But do you want to hear the real bombshell?' Jeff asked. 'My son saw an ambulance and police cars in the lane this morning on his side of the woods. Someone found Fenby in a ditch. Or what was left of him. It looked like he'd been ripped apart – by something.'

Neil stood and sighed as he walked to the window. The mist had lifted now. A soft wind stirred the trees. A single red kite flew high above the woods. Their pheasant woods. Such a peaceful scene.

But there were still secrets out there. Dark secrets… known only to the night – and the silent Hunter's Moon.

Look out for this exciting story
in the *Shades* series:

Penny Bates

Some people said there was no such thing
as Crow Law.

'It's survival of the fittest,' the old man's
daughter liked to say. 'A sick crow is a
danger to the flock and so the others finish
it off. You and your old wives' tales, Dad!'

Only the old man knew better. There
were many trials on Crow Hill. Many small

white skulls now lay beneath the trees. It was the way of crows. They always cast out bad blood.

The young bird didn't move as two crows landed in a rush of black wings. Another shiver ran down the old man's spine. He had seen this before and could not forget how cruel it was. Terror filled the victim's face as the other crows closed in. The guilty crow may have been caught smashing another crow's eggs or killing young in a nest. The other crows would break its wings if they witnessed the crime. Then Crow Law would decide the rest.

The two crows struck first. One crow stood on each side of the bird as they pecked out its eyes. The guilty bird's head jerked from side to side as the crows stabbed and pulled. Then one crow stopped and gave a grisly caw. The blinding was over.

Then the rest of the crows dived down. They threw the bird from side to side. They plucked its feathers and tore strips off its flesh. The old man bit his lip. He prayed for the bird to die fast to end the pain.

'It's not survival of the fittest,' he said, as he watched its skull pecked bare. 'It's revenge!'